LET'S BACK UP!
SPEEDING THROUGH MY FIRST MOVIE

STORY BY PAT CASEY & JOSH MILLER
SCREENPLAY BY PAT CASEY & JOSH MILLER AND JOHN WHITTINGTON
WRITTEN BY JAKE BLACK

PENGUIN YOUNG READERS LICENSES
An imprint of Penguin Random House LLC, New York

First published in the United States of America by Penguin Young Readers Licenses, an imprint of Penguin Random House LLC, New York, 2022

Printed in the United States of America

ISBN 9780593387344   10 9 8 7 6 5 4 3 2 1 COMM

Hi there! My name is Sonic. I grew up on an island on the other side of the universe. I have the ability to run superfast, and I  was supposed to keep that power secret. But I caught the attention of some bad guys who wanted to hurt me. To keep me safe, my guardian, Longclaw, used a ring to send me to Earth.

I arrived on Earth in the town of Green Hills, Montana. It's a beautiful place filled with lots of friendly people. My favorites are the sheriff, who I call "Donut Lord" because he loves to eat donuts, and his wife, who I call "Pretzel Lady" because she twists her body like a pretzel.

Even though I got to know everyone in the town, they didn't know me. I had to stay hidden to be safe. Still, staying hidden made me very lonely.

One night, I was so lonely, I decided to play baseball.
I hit a home run off a pitch I threw myself! As I ran
around the bases, I accidentally ran so fast, I sent out
an energy pulse and knocked out the power for the
entire town!

The government was really mad about the power outage and figured out I had something to do with it. They sent a brilliant-but-evil scientist named Dr. Robotnik to look for me. He had developed amazing robots that would do his bidding and help him capture me—or worse.

I had to leave. Longclaw had given me extra rings that I could use to open a portal to a mushroom planet and escape. I went back to my lair to grab my rings. But before I could open the portal, Robotnik and his drones almost found me!

I ran to the one place I knew I'd be safe: Donut Lord's house. But he found me. I must have scared him, because he hit me with a tranquilizer dart! As I fell asleep, I dropped the rings. They all fell into a portal to San Francisco that I accidentally opened, and landed on top of a building.

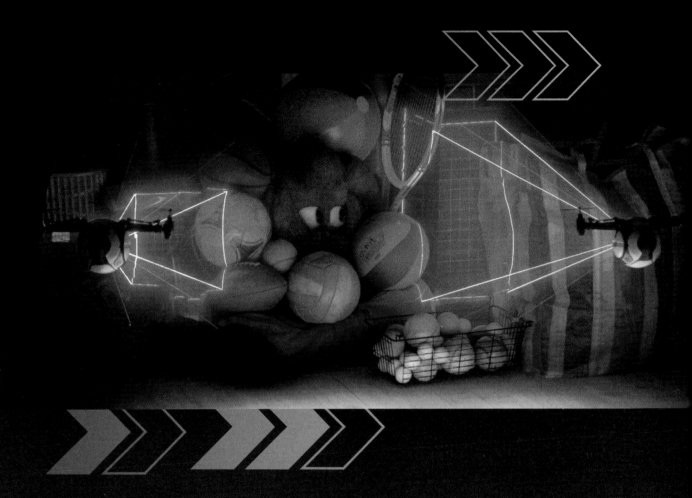

When I woke up, I explained everything to Donut Lord, who agreed to help me. Suddenly, Robotnik showed up at the house looking for me. I hid in the attic while Donut Lord tried to stop Robotnik. Some of Robotnik's drones broke into the attic to look for me!

I rolled into the kitchen, where Robotnik saw me.
Donut Lord grabbed me and carried me outside.
The drones fired their weapons at us as we ran.
I could've taken them all on, but Donut Lord had
other plans. We jumped in his truck and escaped!

Donut Lord refused to go to San Francisco to find my rings. He told me it was west, so I ran west—right into the ocean. I ran back and convinced him to help me get to San Francisco. (But only if I stopped calling him Donut Lord and called him Tom instead.)

We arrived at a cowboy club, one of the coolest places in the world! A bunch of really tough cowboys were eating food and fighting.

Donut Lor—I mean, Tom, had to make a phone call to the sheriff's office. I guess he talked to Robotnik, who told him he was going to find us, because when Tom got back, he was a little freaked out.

I was supposed to stay in the truck, but I couldn't help myself! I went into the cowboy club. Tom followed me in, and one of the cowboys didn't like us too much and told us to leave. I didn't want to, so I started a huge fight, but escaped with Tom before we got hurt.

I was so excited from the fight at the cowboy club, I just wanted to keep going and going! See, I had this list of everything I wanted to do on Earth before I left for the Mushroom Planet and had checked a bunch of them off in just one day. What a great day!

The next morning, Tom and I continued on our way to San Francisco. Suddenly, Robotnik found us in this, like, high-tech tank! He hooked onto us with a cable, and we couldn't get away.

Robotnik sent his drones to attack us. Tom and I fought them off. A tiny one cut off the entire top of the truck! Tom had me drive while he fought Robotnik and the drones.

We escaped from Robotnik and the drones, but I discovered one was stuck to me. Just as we got it off, it exploded and sent us flying through the air.

Tom drove us the rest of the way to San Francisco and took us to Pretzel Lady (I guess her name is actually Maddie), who was visiting her sister. Maddie's an animal doctor and was able to help me feel better after the explosion, and her niece gave me some awesome sneakers to run in.

Tom and Maddie figured out which building my rings fell on. They sneaked me into the building in a really tiny bag and got me to the roof. I found my rings and said goodbye to Tom and Maddie. But just as I was about to leave for the Mushroom Planet, Robotnik appeared in a weird spaceship thing!

I quickly sent Tom and Maddie to safety back in Green Hills and began to fight back against Robotnik. My superspeed was faster than his missiles, and I used that to my advantage, catching them and sending them flying back at Robotnik.

He chased me all through San Francisco, blowing up stuff, but he couldn't hit me! He followed me all over the world. I saw the Eiffel Tower, the Pyramids of Giza, and everything! Finally, we ended up back in Green Hills.

watched me battle Robotnik. He was ranting on and on about how I don't belong here or something. I used my superspeed to hit his ship from every direction. I even caused another energy pulse, disabling his ship! Before he could crash, I used a ring to open up a portal and send him away.

The portal I sent Dr. Robotnik through took him to the Mushroom Planet. I'm so happy we got rid of that guy and his egg-shaped drones. Maybe I'll call him Dr. Eggman from now on!

Tom and Maddie let me live in their attic. It is so nice not to have to hide from the people I love anymore. They gave me a home. And the best part is, I'm not lonely anymore!

Still, I can't help but wonder what's in store for us. Who knows what might happen next . . .

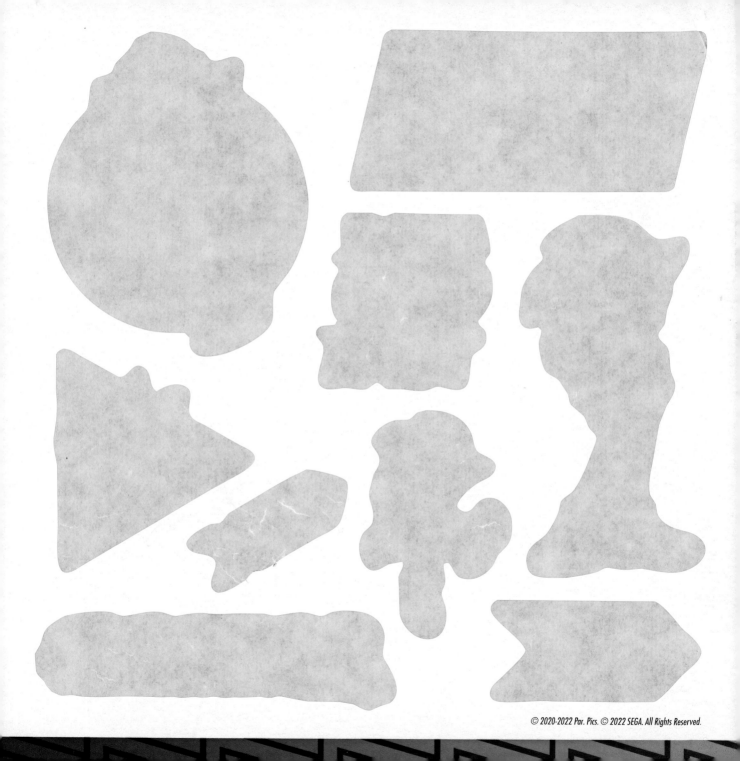